**FRIENDS
OF ACPL**

W9-BCM-913

Bullfrog Builds a House

by **Rosamond Dauer**
illustrated by **Byron Barton**

Greenwillow
Read-alone

GREENWILLOW BOOKS
A Division of William Morrow & Company, Inc.
New York

Library of Congress Cataloging in Publication Data

Dauer, Rosamond.
Bullfrog builds a house.
(Greenwillow read-alone series)
Summary: Not wanting to forget any important items in
his new house, Bullfrog seeks the advice of Gertrude.
Upon completion he finds he has overlooked one thing.
[1. Frogs—Fiction. 2. Friendship—Fiction]
I. Barton, Byron. II. Title. PZ7.D2615Bs [E]
76-54820 ISBN 0-688-80090-4 ISBN 0-688-84090-6 lib. bdg.

For Gertrude Sterling Mueller

Bullfrog
looked and looked
until he found
a large lake.

8

"Just right!" he said.

"I will live here."

And he set out

to build a house.

But he wasn't quite sure

where to start.

As Bullfrog sat on a log

to eat his lunch and think,

another frog

came out of the bushes.

"And who are you?"

Bullfrog asked.

"My name is Gertrude,"

said the other frog.

"An excellent name,"

said Bullfrog.

"Will you share my lunch?"

"Yes, thank you,"
said Gertrude,
and she ate just as much
as Bullfrog.

Bullfrog was impressed.

"You have a good appetite,"

he said.

"Oh, indeed I have,"

said Gertrude.

"Since you have an appetite
like mine," said Bullfrog,
"perhaps you can tell me
how to begin my new house."

"That's easy," said Gertrude.

"Start with what you like best."

"A diving board
   on the front porch!"
   said Bullfrog.
"I've always wanted
   to have one."
"What wonderful ideas
   you have!" said Gertrude.
"I must start at once,"
   said Bullfrog.
   And he did.

He built a porch

in no time at all,

and started to work

on his diving board.

But he was soon in trouble.

"Ah, Gertrude," he said,

"would you mind

standing in the water

to balance the board

so I can nail it in?"

"Not at all," said Gertrude,

and she held up the board

for Bullfrog.

23

"Very good," said Bullfrog

when they were finished.

"And now," he said,

"I will build

the rest of the house."

As time went by,

Gertrude helped Bullfrog

with many things.

They put a stove
in the kitchen,
a bathtub
in the bathroom,
and a table
in the living room.

Finally Bullfrog and Gertrude

stepped back

to admire their work.

"Wonderful!" said Bullfrog.

"But have I forgotten

something?"

"My dear Bullfrog,"
said Gertrude,
"it is a beautiful house,
but may I suggest
a roof?"

30

"Oh, good friend,"

said Bullfrog,

"you think of everything!"

Then Gertrude and Bullfrog

put a roof on the house.

When they were finished,

Bullfrog said,

"Now there is just

one more thing, I think."

"And what is that?"
asked Gertrude.
"A welcome mat!"
said Bullfrog.
"That would be nice,"
Gertrude said.
So Bullfrog
put out a welcome mat.

33

"NOW," said Bullfrog,

"I have everything

  I need!"

"BUT," said Gertrude,

"isn't there something else?"

"I don't think so,"

  said Bullfrog.

"Well," said Gertrude,

"in that case,

I must be leaving."

"Good-by," said Bullfrog.

"Thank you for helping

to build my house."

"You are welcome,"

said Gertrude. "Good-by."

And Gertrude went away.

Then Bullfrog

looked at his house.

He thought about having

a good dive

off the diving board,

but didn't feel like it.

He felt a little hungry,
but didn't want to fix
a hamburger.

He went upstairs to look
at his new bathtub,
but he didn't take a bath.

He started to play cards,

but couldn't think of a game

for just one frog.

"What is the matter?"
wondered Bullfrog.
"I must be getting a cold."
So Bullfrog wrapped up
in a big blanket,
but he still
didn't feel just right.

43

Suddenly he jumped up.

"GERTRUDE! GERTRUDE!"

he shouted.

And he ran down the road

in his blanket

until he found Gertrude.

"What is the matter?"

asked Gertrude.

"Oh, well . . ." said Bullfrog.

"That is, I wondered . . .

I mean . . . " and Bullfrog stopped.

"Oh dear," said Gertrude,

"do you have a cold?"

"NO!" said Bullfrog.
"I just wondered
    if you would care
    to . . . play cards."

"Oh yes," said Gertrude.

"Good," said Bullfrog.

50

And Gertrude and Bullfrog
went back to Bullfrog's house
to play cards.

Later, Gertrude
taught Bullfrog
how to play checkers.
"Oh," said Bullfrog,
"you are a fine frog!

How fortunate I am

to have you with me!"

"Of course," said Gertrude.

"I am happy to be here."

54

"You must stay forever!"

said Bullfrog.

"I would like that very much,"

said Gertrude.

"Now, how about a game

of touch football?"

"Wonderful!" cried Bullfrog.

And Bullfrog and Gertrude

were very happy

in their beautiful house

from then on.